Judith Mathews

AN EGG and SEVEN SOCKS

Illustrated by Marylin Hafner

HarperCollinsPublishers

For Shel, and for all my fellow silly sisters
—J.M.

To my friend Elissa, with love
—M.H.

Note: *When people darned (or repaired) torn clothing by hand, they sometimes used a darning "egg." They held the egg—not a* real *egg, just a hard, egg-shaped object— underneath the cloth with the hole on top; then they wove the torn threads together with a needle.*

In a small village lived three foolish sisters named Lacey, Doily, and Thimblethreads. They knew how to do only one thing— that was to darn socks.

One bright morning, each sister sat down, put a wooden darning egg into a sock
with a hole in it, and began to sew up the hole. Suddenly, a terrible wind came out
of the east. It rushed in through an open window and rushed out again.

Lacey, the eldest and bravest, jumped from her seat. "The wind has stolen our socks!" she cried angrily. "Seven of them—I counted!"

"What would it want with seven old socks?" asked Doily.

"Heaven's cold clocks!" chimed Thimblethreads. "Heaven's cold clocks!" For she could only speak in rhyme.

"Right!" said Lacey. "The clocks in heaven are cold and need socks to keep them warm." And she sat down again.

But Thimblethreads burst into tears. Her sisters looked at her and gasped—Thimblethreads's darning egg was gone!

"We must get that egg back!" said Lacey. "It came from MOTHER! We will follow the wind to the west," she declared.

The next morning, the sisters left, taking with them needles and thread and all their socks full of holes.

Rounding a curve, they came upon a sad-looking donkey.

"Look!" cried Doily. "A poor, homeless creature."

"Come along," said Lacey. "We must be on our way."

But the donkey followed them. "Hee-haw-hee-haw-hee-haw-hee," he said when he caught up with the travelers.

"Haw-hee!" said Lacey. "What a pretty name." They decorated the donkey with their best socks, put the rest of their belongings onto his sturdy back, and went on.

Soon they came to a town in the center of which stood a great castle. Many of the buildings around the castle were crumbled to bits, and the people huddled sadly together.

"So this is how people live in cities," said Lacey. "How lucky we are that in our village the houses stand up straight."

Now it happened that the king of the land was walking along the battlements of his castle, unhappily looking over the town, when he saw the sisters and their dressed-up donkey. "I could use some silliness, to take my mind off my worries," thought he. He called down to his guards, "Invite them in! Have their donkey fed and bring those women to see me!"

When the sisters came before the king, Lacey spoke. "I am Lacey, this is Doily, and that is Thimblethreads, your Kingship."

The king wanted to laugh out loud. Instead he asked, "Tell me, fair ladies, what brings you here?"

"Dearest Majesty," Lacey began, "yesterday, we were sitting in our cottage, as right as ever, when the wind came and stole seven socks—"

"For the clocks! For the clocks!" chimed Thimblethreads.

"The socks went to heaven," said Doily, "but the wind has Sister's darning egg—"

"—and we must get it back," cried Lacey, "because it came from MOTHER!"

The king's eyes twinkled and his belly shook. "You have told a fine tale," he said, "and for that you shall have some dinner."

After the sisters had eaten, the king
bade them farewell. "I warn you, do not
travel westward," he said. "The terrible
dragon that destroyed our town lives that
way." But the sisters just smiled at him.

"We've never met a dragon who did us
any harm," said Lacey.

"We've never met a dragon at all!" said
Doily. And with that, the sisters waved
good-bye.

BE CAREFUL!

Lacey, Doily, Thimblethreads, and Haw-hee went westward for some time until they came to a great, dark cave. From its mouth a foul smell poured forth.

"Ugh! Someone hold my nose, please," said Doily.

"The hideout of a rotten cheese!" declared Thimblethreads.

"A very strong rotten cheese," said Lacey, "and a very suspicious one." She entered the cave and the others followed her.

Soon enough, they discovered the cave's owner, who was not a cheese...

…but a dragon.

"Ho there," said the dragon, heaving himself to his feet. "You seem good to eat!"

"Look!" cried Doily, pointing to a great, messy pile. "There are our socks! Are we in heaven? Or did you steal them from the wind?"

"You fool, I *made* the wind. Those socks just blew in from who knows where."

"You made the wind?" cried Doily. "Then *you* are the thief!" She peered beneath the dragon's belly. "And you're trying to hatch Sister's darning egg, too."

"Give it back," said Lacey. "It's ours."

"Finders keepers," said the dragon nastily. "And, since I have found *you*, I'll keep you, too!" The dragon licked his lips. "One blast of fire and you'll all be cooked!" he boomed. Then he opened his enormous mouth—but Haw-hee turned around and kicked him hard on the snout. The dragon roared in pain.

"Quick!" shouted Lacey. "Stop that dragon!"

"How? How?" cried Doily.

Thimblethreads jumped forward. "Hand in sock!" she cried. "Foot in glove. Use what we have plenty of!"

"Of course!" said Lacey, and they started throwing socks at the dragon.

The dragon gasped for breath—and found a sock caught in his throat. "Darn it! Darn this sock!" he tried to say, but he couldn't speak. The dragon coughed. He choked and gasped. He rasped and roared and coughed some more. And then, with a terrible crash, he fell down dead.

"A pity!" said Doily. "It was such a pretty sock."

"Look—we have the egg that came from MOTHER!" cried Lacey. "And because we are dragon slayers, we get to keep all this gold, too. We can use our socks to carry it home."

"But the socks have holes in them," said Doily.

"Then we must darn them," said Lacey.

And that is what they did, though it took them days and days.

At last, they put everything on Haw-hee's back and off they went.

When they arrived at the castle, the king came out to greet them. "Did you get all your things from the wind?" he asked.

"Yes," said Doily, "and also the gold from the dragon's cave."

"The dragon!" said the king. "Did you slay him with a sword?"

"No," said Lacey, "we slew him with a sock." She tossed two gold-filled socks at the king. "Now you can fix up your funny town," she told him.

"I shall do that," the king said, smiling. "But first, I'll have a celebration to honor the great dragon slayers!"

And he did.

The next morning, the sisters bade farewell to the king and all the townspeople.

As soon as they arrived home, they fed Haw-hee some nice hay. Then they went inside, sat right down, and began to mend socks. When the sun set, they all got ready for bed. "Sisters," said Doily, "we are rich now. Why are we working so hard?"

"Well," said Lacey, "we may have lots of gold, but there is still only one thing we know how to do. Am I not right?"

"Good night! Good night! As we turn out the light!" sang Thimblethreads.

And they did.

Library of Congress Cataloging-in-Publication Data
Mathews, Judith.
     An egg and seven socks / by Judith Mathews ; pictures by Marylin
Hafner.
          p.   cm.
     Summary: Three silly sisters, who earn their living darning socks,
go on a journey to recover seven socks and a darning egg, and meet a
king and a dragon.
     ISBN 0-06-020207-6. — ISBN 0-06-020208-4 (lib. bdg.)
     [1. Socks—Fiction. 2. Dragons—Fiction.] I. Hafner, Marylin,
ill. II. Title. III. Title: Egg and 7 socks.
PZ7.M42517Eg   1993   91-11476
[E]—dc20   CIP
                                                                        AC